"The soul of a story." No five words can better describe Kelly Maurica's approach to capturing the heart and soul of a story.

But who is Kelly Maurica?

Kelly spent the majority of her career working as a nurse. Full of creativity and passion for writing and storytelling, Kelly longed to tell the stories of connection. Kelly believes that by sharing stories of resilience, heartache, love, and joy she empowers her readers to discover something: a moment of connectedness.

Only by viewing circumstances through the lens of another person can we learn to empathize with others and discover that we are not walking alone.

Born and raised in Toronto, Ontario, Kelly now spends her time in Calgary, Alberta enjoying life's simple pleasures— long drives that lead to nowhere, spending time with her family, and sipping wine on her deck.

For my friends and family, you inspire my creativity.

For my two boys, who I love more than anything in this world. The two of you make me a better mom, writer, storyteller and friend.

For the man of my dreams, I am so glad we met.

KELLY MAURICA

STORIES WITH SOLE

AUSTIN MACAULEY PUBLISHERS™

LONDON • CAMBRIDGE • NEW YORK • SHARJAH

Ordering Information
Quantity sales: Special discounts are available on quantity purchases by corporations, associations, and others. For details, contact the publisher at the address below.

Publisher's Cataloging-in-Publication data
Maurica, Kelly
Stories with Sole

ISBN 9781643789545 (Paperback)
ISBN 9781645365327 (ePub e-book)

Library of Congress Control Number: 2022900914

www.austinmacauley.com/us

First Published 2022
Austin Macauley Publishers LLC
40 Wall Street, 33rd Floor, Suite 3302
New York, NY 10005
USA

mail-usa@austinmacauley.com
+1 (646) 5125767

A special note…

For the beautiful souls, the dreamers, and the creators.

For those who struggle with life daily but who still find the courage to give 100% of themselves and carry on.

For those who have experienced joy, laughter, heartache, pain, despair, love, and sorrow.

For those who share a piece of themselves, with their whole heart every day.

For the women of the 'Patchwork Project', you are my muses and I adore each one of you.

And for J. Iron Word, whose quotes added that missing piece to the heart and soul of these stories.

Eternal Love, Grace, and Gratitude,

Kelly

"What if my heart stopped, would my soul cease to exist, or would it still live by the same rhythm and beat it has always lived by?"

– *J. Iron Word*

As she sat down and placed the aluminum foil pan on the blanket beside her, she allowed her bare feet to run across the warm, moist blades of the grass beneath her feet. She looked up at the cloudless sky and noticed how the vibrant shade of blue filled every corner of the heavens above. It appeared to her that on this particular day, the sky was bluer than she had ever noticed before. She saw lots of things lately, simple things. She leaned back – all the way back, closed her eyes, and slowly inhaled. She could smell the scent of lavender and mimosa, and she was thankful for Mrs. Mulligan's butterfly garden, filled with its multiple hues of pink, red and yellow wildflowers, not only did that garden explode with color but the scents from all the competing flowers were enough to bring a smile to her face.

As she laid in the middle of her backyard, the hot sun beating down on her face, she thought about all of the little things that she would miss. The handwritten birthday cards written in crayon, cuddling on the sofa with her twin girls –

her nose nuzzled in the nape of their necks, sipping a cup of hot ginger tea while watching the morning sun peek through the branches, and snuggling in her husband's arms on the bathroom floor after yet another painful sleepless night.

The cancer had changed her. All the little things that most people took for granted daily were now a constant reminder of how precious life was. She hated that she was now at the point where she was referring to life in the past tense, but it was – it is her reality. The doctors had given her three months left to live after the last round of chemotherapy, and each day was a blessing. She was thankful for this last.

She was grateful to be able to say goodbye to all the people that mattered. Cancer was a cold-hearted son of a bitch, but it had given her this time to pause. She had spent the morning writing the girls letters for each milestone that she was going to miss all the firsts. The first dance, the first kiss, the first broken heart, and watching from the pew as her first daughter walked down the aisle. As she laid on her back in her backyard, she was ready to fill the afternoon sky with as many gratitude bubbles that her tired body would allow. She dipped the tiny plastic pink wand into the soapy mixture and raised the baton to her lips. She uttered a big thank you and blew.

"The rarest flowers stand out, because they grow and thrive despite their surroundings."

— *J. Iron Word*

It had been two years—two years—since that day, and two years since life as I had known it had changed. My world had changed. I never thought I would have made it through the darkness and the despair, but here I am, recovered, healthy, and alive.

Two years ago, I had strapped on my backpack, wrote a note to my boyfriend, taped it to our usual spot on the fridge, right below the cheesy picture of the two of us at a photo booth. The photo booth that we had discovered while on a road trip through Utah.

We had stumbled upon a diner in the middle of nowhere. In the corner of the restaurant was this photo booth, equipped with the red velvet curtain and corresponding red velvet backdrop. It looked like it had not been used in years, but Stan put in two quarters, and we made the funniest faces that we could think of as the bulbs flashed their blinding light.

I had always craved adventure, and most of the time my experiences led us on various road trips to explore, hike, rock climb, and hang glide. The more dangerous the activity, the better. There was no better feeling than the rush of adrenaline coursing through my body as I climbed or jumped off the tallest mountain, glided over the deepest gorge, or hiked off the beaten path. I was always pushing my boundaries and looking for that next big rush.

I knew that perhaps squirrel parachuting alone was not the smartest option, but no one wanted to participate in my daredevil activities. Stan, the love of my life and my usual companion had to work, and I really didn't want to let a gorgeous day like today pass me by.

I closed the apartment door, grabbed my bike, and placed it on the bike rack on the back of my truck. I jumped in the vehicle, turned up the Big Chill soundtrack that was playing on my iPod, and started to drive north toward the pristine mountains. I would park, then bike to the base of the mountain, hike up, and then glide down. I had completed this trek many times before so I knew exactly where I would land – give or take.

When I finally hiked to the peak, three hours later, I stood and admired the weather conditions. It was such a beautiful day. There was a breeze, and the sun was beginning to dry the dew on my feet.

Excellent, I thought.

By my calculations at this altitude and wind speed, the wind would gently guide me to the bottom of the valley, within the approximate location where I had left my bike. I checked my squirrel suit for any tears, strapped in, and jumped. It had been the perfect dismount, and the glide was peaceful. The earth beneath me appeared insignificant, and I enjoyed the serenity.

As I glided effortlessly toward the ground, I saw the clouds peeking from behind the mountain, birds appeared suspended in flight, and the air smelled and felt crisp and clean. Then out of nowhere, a gust of wind blew me off course. I tried to regain control, but I was unable to navigate myself back to that calm soar. I lost control and eventually slammed into the mountain and lost consciousness. When I finally woke, I thought I was dead.

There was no possible way I could have survived that fall, but there I was in the hospital, tubes everywhere. I had six broken ribs, a chest tube was sticking out from my chest draining blood-tinged fluid and attempting to keep my collapsed lung inflated. A tube drained urine from my bladder, and a constant and annoying beeping filled the room.

Day-in and day-out I lay flat on my back, staring up at a clinical white, florescent illuminated ceiling filled with ceiling tiles that housed a multitude of tiny holes. Day after day, I counted the number of holes that were in each tile across the entire ceiling above my head. When I finished counting, I would start all over again. The halo traction that had been screwed into my skull prevented me from turning my head.

The nurses had to turn me as a unit, and it generally took four or five nurses to make sure that my limbs, head, and body moved in unison. The daily round of doctors uttered words like—*lucky to be alive, it's a miracle that she was found, at least she has her life.*

One day the pain in my left leg was excruciating. I reached down to rub my thigh but only felt a stump. I screamed over and over again, I kept screaming. The nurses frantically tried to console me and finally resorted to injecting me with a sedative to help settle my panic. I found out later that the coyotes had eaten away the majority of the flesh from my shattered leg. It was indeed a miracle that I did not bleed to death, and it was either sheer luck or God Himself who had sent the group of students to the exact location where my unconscious and battered body was found. If it weren't for their field trip, I would not be alive today.

Rehab was painful. I had to re-learn the mechanics of sitting, walking, dressing, and feeding myself. There were so many days where I had wanted to give up and so many more days that I wished I had died. I spent seven days a week in physiotherapy, cursing my therapist, but she did not give up on me. Perhaps it was the determination that helped me build the strength to carry on, or maybe it was because my boyfriend Stan had proposed to me as I laid crying in a puddle on the mat inside the hospital gym. I became determined to live the life that I was spared. Sure, I no longer had a left leg, but I was alive.

Today I look down at my left leg, propped up on my beaten leather sofa, grateful for how far I have progressed. A year ago, I didn't think that I would have made it this far, and two years ago on that fateful day, I could not have imagined that I would have survived, but here I sit, intact except for a prosthetic left leg.

I slipped on my Barre sock and Birkenstock, ready to conquer my next adventure – dance lessons for my upcoming wedding.

"How many yesterdays have you spent your todays on?
How many tomorrows have slipped through your fingers
while you were focused on what can never change?"

— *J. Iron Word*

The infertility treatments had led to seven miscarriages and diagnosis of a *non-viable uterus. Non-viable.*

Apparently, my womb was incapable of carrying another lifeform inside of it. Fertilized eggs would implant, but my uterus would reject the new being as it attempted to further attach, form, and grow inside me. We finally decided to stop the fertility treatments and looked into adoption.

Adoption was a long and arduous process, and when couples wanted a baby as opposed to a toddler or child, the process was more daunting. We had finally been chosen as successful prospective parents, only to have the anonymous mother decide that she no longer wanted to hand her baby over to strangers.

Strangers – we were not strangers. Jacob was a prominent cardiac surgeon, and I was a fifth-grade teacher. We were contributing members of society, and we cared about humanity. I volunteered on the weekends at the local battered women's shelter. Jacob spent a month every year in Haiti, volunteering his time and expertise for Doctors Without Borders. We gave – not only money – but our time to helping others less fortunate than us. We would have been great parents, but apparently, the Universe did not agree. I sat barren, hoping that one day, I too would be blessed with a child.

I had given up hope on ever hearing the pitter-patter of little feet running across the well-maintained hardwood floor. Every year at Christmas, I watched the frazzled parents fight over the newest video game and doll of the year, wishing that I was part of the pre-Christmas chaos.

Year after year, the crib sat empty. I became tired of trying. Jacob was an amazing husband and stood by my side throughout all of it, but I had to face the fact – a baby was not meant to be. I resigned myself to my reality; I was a school teacher, and perhaps everyone else's children somehow belonged to me – at least for eight hours out of the day. I threw myself into my work and vowed to make a difference for all the boys and girls that entered my classroom.

One day as I finally packed all of my hopes and dreams into several cardboard boxes, I gifted the stained mahogany crib to my best friend; who was now pregnant with twins. I realized that I could not bring myself to throw away the tiny ballet slippers that had belonged to me when I was a child. My mother had kept them in pristine condition, and I kept them in a small pink plastic ballet case in the attic.

That was four years ago. I now sit at the back of Miss Julie's ballet studio, watching all the tiny kids try to plie, pirouette, and stand straight with their heads held high. One little girl escaped the group and came running my way.

"Mommy, Mommy, did you see me? Did you see me do my spin?"

"Of course, sweet pea! But you should get back to the group, you don't want to keep Miss Julie waiting."

"Okay mommy, but watch me okay?"

Janna blew me a kiss and flitted away.

Jacob was no longer with us. A drunk driver had taken his life four years earlier, as he drove to the hospital to prepare a patient for a heart transplant. His death saved two people that night, and he left me the best parting gift-a viable pregnancy that ultimately formed the sweetest, most loving strawberry blonde girl-the same girl, now wearing the ballet slippers that I could not bring myself to throw away.

"Music often accompanies me, my thoughts, my mood, my silence."

— *J. Iron Word*

The year was 1978, and the disco was alive.

It was the era of big hair, big red lips, short skirts, and free love. Everyone, no matter who you were, what you did for a living, or where you lived, looked forward to Friday night. When the clock struck five, the city came alive with a sea of people, all racing home to get ready for a night filled with endless possibilities.

New York City was the place to be, and the dance clubs were the place to be seen. Studio fifty-four was the hottest nightclub in Manhattan. Once you walked through that door, you couldn't help but feel the music hit you in your soul. The bass coursed through your body and appeared to keep rhythm with the beating of your heart.

Disco balls, with their endless mirrors and psychedelic lights, illuminated the entire club and everyone – I mean everyone – was dressed to impress. Bell bottom jeans, hot pants, peek-a-boo crochet tops were revealing without being offensive. It was live and let live and the only goal of the night was to dance your ass off.

I danced the whole night away until I couldn't feel my feet, and then I danced some more. Swaying and gyrating my hips. The sweat pouring off my body. At the end of the night, I grabbed my shoes in one hand, and my handsome dancing partner in the other and headed back home.

"One of my favorite things about us is being able to pick up where we left off. No matter the time between us, it is almost as if we have been there all along."

– J. Iron Word

The year was 1932, and Geneviève was the most beautiful woman that I had ever seen. Her long curly hair was deep black. Black like the coal that was extracted from the depths of the mine in town. Her cheeks were a constant hue of life that exuded warmth, and when she laughed her brown eyes sparkled as bright as my mother's expensive jewels that she kept locked in her bedroom safe. Genevive's chocolate brown skin always glowed richly with love, tenderness, and integrity.

I loved Geneviève from the first moment I saw her. I wanted to know her, and that's where our story began. Geneviève had worked for my father tending to his garden, so it was easy to talk with her. It was 1932, and while my father had hired a Negro, he had no tolerance for their kind, as he said.

According to father, the only thing the Negros were good for was cooking, cleaning, tending to gardens, and making babies. I did not share in my father's antiquated and prejudiced opinions. Mamie, my Negro nanny was the kindest, gentlest, most tolerant person I had known. She had taught me that people were people no matter the color of their skin and that the real test of a person's character was in how they treated one another. The words they chose showed their honesty and integrity.

Mamie taught me that people who were kind to your face should never be trusted and that people who had to *dress up* their communication always had something to hide. Mamie also taught me that honesty, transparency, and directness were cherished over, trying to say things correctly. "Say what you mean, and you will always be respected. People's feelings may get hurt boy, but they will respect you."

I found myself quite taken with Mamie's niece Geneviève, twice removed on her mother's side. I would try to take long leisurely strolls through the garden, pretending that I was reading from my favorite poetry book. I spent hours under the hot sun helping Darius dig wells for the irrigation system that my father had planned to install for the garden that Geneviève was hired to tend.

One day Geneviève had bought the most fantastic array of brightly colored purple flowers–purple she said, like the purple cravat and blue suede shoes that she said she liked to see me wearing, was the color of wisdom, independence, and strength, qualities she believed I possessed.

The year was 1932, and our love was forbidden. We had to be careful, this we knew. Our friendship had quickly blossomed into a passion, and we were always pretending that our meetings were a mere business arrangement-no one could know, for if they did, it would mean death for both of us. Our love grew stronger with each passing season, but so did the bigotry, racism, and ignorance.

Two years after I had met Geneviève, my father secured a job as a banker in Charlotte, North Carolina, and my family moved away. I dated several high society women, women my parents approved of, but none of them compared to Geneviève, and in the end, I married another.

I had lived a full life with Joanna, and I did love her. We had raised four exceptional children, and when Joanna died, I mourned her. When I could no longer live in the house that Joanna and I shared, I moved into a retirement center, and I now spend my days reminiscing about days gone by, missed opportunities, and my very first love, Geneviève.

Two months ago, I saw them – a multitude of brightly colored purple flowers, planted in the center of the courtyard.

It's April 5, 2019, and we are getting married, surrounded by family and friends and a multitude of purple flowers. I'm wearing a similar purple cravat and blue suede shoes that I had been wearing the moment I first saw her.

"Fragile comes in many forms, and she is the most delicate thing that has ever been broken, but is now the strongest because of it."

— *J. Iron Word*

Andrea looked around her home. The home that she had made for herself and her daughter and to some extent, her husband. Lyle had been deployed for parts unknown two years ago, and she didn't know when or if he would return, although every night she prayed that he would return safely.

That was the reality of being a service wife. Service wives created a life and a dwelling so that the one person who was dedicated to preserving freedom for so many others had a safe haven to call home. A place filled with love and laughter.

Hurricane Rodolfo was descending down on the Carolina coast, and Andrea had to make a tough decision. Stay and confront Rodolfo head-on and hope that she and her daughter could survive its wrath or bravely take her daughter by the hand, grab the two emergency backpacks that she had prepared filled with only the bare necessities, and walk away. Andrea knew that it would be difficult to walk away. As Andrea stood in the middle of the once active living room, she remembered the many Christmases that were spent hanging stockings over the fireplace and the bedtime stories that had been read underneath the covers in Charlotte's brightly painted pink room. She knew every nook and cranny of this house, especially the many secret places to hide during extensive games of hide and seek.

This home was filled with memories, and it was the home where Charlotte had been born, right in the middle of the living room, in an inflatable kiddie pool filled with warm water surrounded by the other service wives and her midwife, while Lyle watched from the screen on someone's iPad. These were the memories that she didn't want to let go. Not yet anyway and not under such dire circumstances. Andrea turned back to listen to the weather forecast on her television. The storm was coming, and she knew it was time to decide; stay and risk her life and the life of her daughter or go and never see this home again.

Leaving was the decision she made a week ago. The base had called and said that she could return to remove any items that she saw fit, but that she could no longer live there. The storm had blown through the area with such force, causing mass flooding in many areas. Her home, while still standing, was no longer habitable.

When Andrea entered the house for the first time since she left, she immediately noticed the destruction. Watermarks were evident from where the water level had been receding. She walked into what was once her living room, and while the water level was now low, she still had to walk through water that was ankle-deep. Charlotte's toys were floating aimlessly amongst the debris and filth, and she gasped as she saw Charlotte's favorite doll Trixie, float by.

The ceiling was burst open to reveal a mixture of dirty water and black mold. Everything from photographs – that had been left hanging on the walls to all of Charlotte's clothes, toys, and stuffed animals were destroyed. She didn't want to continue to walk through the building she had once called home.

So many memories were now soaked with water and despair. She opened her bedroom closet and there sitting on the top shelf were a pair of her husbands' boots, the same pair that he had worn in the 4th of July parade, the day before he was deployed. That was such a great day. They had been so happy, positive, and safe. Not a care in the world. She wondered if she would ever feel that level of safety again. The world was an unpredictable place, and with the experience of now having to put her life back together thanks to the unpredictability of mother nature, she didn't know if she had the strength to carry on. She picked up the boots from the shelf, the flag still protruding from the laces just as Lyle had left them.

In that instant, she realized that she was lucky to be alive. Andrea had kept her daughter safe, and they had an opportunity to carry on when so many others were not as fortunate. She cuddled the wet boots close to her chest, wiped the tears from her eyes, and walked out the front door, her head held high. She was determined to carry on and not look back.

"It seems that those with the biggest hearts are the first to go almost as if they know and they love enough for a lifetime in less than a blink."

— *J. Iron Word*

In the bowels of the earth, there is an inner-city known as the mine. A place shrouded in blackness, consumed by dampness, and where the air is stagnant.

The mine is a modern-day representation of what one might imagine of a post-apocalyptic world. There is no greenery, no freshness, and the only light that is present beams from the artificial fluorescent lamp strapped to our hard hats. Yet every day, at the crack of dawn, we pull on our boots, button up our coveralls and descend into the pit in which we make a living. We are like ants, working each day diligently extracting the one commodity that continues to be in high demand – oil.

Cole and I were sitting eating lunch, in the same spot that we had eaten lunch for the past ten years. The cold, damp floor of the mine served as our picnic area, and our knees served as our table. We were talking about our football pool and trying to determine if either one of us would make any money in the draft this year. I was about to take another bite of the meatloaf sandwich that Jillian, my wife, had made last evening when I heard the first crack. I stopped and listened. The mine was filled with sounds. The buzz of the generator, the whirl of a drill, the shattering of rocks, but this sound was different. I sat listening for another minute when I heard the second crack, my eyes locked immediately with Cole, and I saw the terror in his eyes.

"We have to move now!" Cole yelled.

We frantically grabbed our harnesses, left our lunch on the ground, and began to run. It was dark, and when you have nearly fifty men all fleeing a tiny cave in the dark, navigation was not easy, even with our headlamps.

At first, small shards of rock broke loose from the walls of the shaft. Then more enormous rocks started to rain down on the men around us. We dodged and weaved both men and rocks. As men fell, we all wanted to stop and help, but the panic turned into a frenzy, and the only mission was to reach the elevator and to get out.

Men were pushing their way through others and onto the elevator in the distance. We had to make it or die trying. As I reached the elevator shaft, I heard Cole scream. I turned and saw a wooden scaffolding beam dislodge from the wall and penetrate Cole's shoulder. He dropped. I stopped turned around, and grabbed Cole by the legs, and dragged him the rest of the way. The elevator was filling fast, but I was able to wedge myself in and pull Cole up into the hoist in front of me.

"I'm closing the gate, I can't let any more on. If there are too many people, we won't move," yelled Justin, the elevator operator. I looked at the men who didn't get on and wondered if I would ever see them again. Justin pushed the button, and we slowly started to rise. Rocks from the shaft began to break loose around us at lightning speed. The cave was imploding on itself, and we had to get out.

It was challenging to hold onto Cole, he had been pushed to the edge of the elevator. I could see him holding his shoulder with a large piece of the beam sticking out. I untied my vest and managed to tie a makeshift tourniquet around his shoulder, attempting to secure both the bleeding and the scaffold in place. We locked eyes once again, and I patted him on his other shoulder.

Cole had been my best friend since grade three, and I wasn't letting him go. Rock fragments continued to hit the elevator cage causing the hoist to sway from side to side. Then, a large boulder hit the cage, I lost my footing, and I also lost my hold on Cole. Cole buckled backward and fell over the side. I grabbed his boot, but it was too late, he fell back down into the mine and possibly to his death as I ascended to safety.

Cole had been my best friend since grade three, the best man at my wedding, and now I had to tell his wife and three boys that he would not be coming home for supper tonight.

"I took a walk down memory lane today, for the first time in years. It was longer than I remembered, but every bit as beautiful as when you were still here."

— *J. Iron Word*

The years had gone by fast; too fast.

I remembered his first birthday. His first birthday party with that Wall-E cake covered in blue icing that when eaten had made all the kids look like they needed oxygen on account of their blue lips. Then there was the trip to Los Angeles that we took when he was eleven. He loved the excitement of Venice Beach, the ice cream sundae that we ate on the makeshift patio on Hollywood Boulevard, and the long walks we took at dusk through unfamiliar neighborhoods.

He had his first drink – a glass of wine a few weeks ago when he turned nineteen and woke up with his first hangover the next day. I took him to the neighborhood diner for his first big plate of greasy restaurant food – hangover food. There had been so many firsts, and now this first was bittersweet. Here I was, packing up his room and preparing him for his first experience away from home. He was moving out and moving away to attend college on the other side of the country.

I looked down at the lone pair of shoes kicked under the bed. I had become accustomed to seeing the five or six pairs of shoes stacked haphazardly at the front door that had been a constant reminder of a full house. The boys, his friends, had been a regular fixture at our house over the years. I would come home from work to a house full of laughter, wrestling, and the occasional fight. The gossip about who was dating, who filtered up through the vents, and I heard every word. My fridge had to be full of food for his growing group of friends – friends who were now all moving away to begin their own adult lives.

I looked down once again at the lone converse laying on its side by his bed. I walked over to the window and watched my son, packing the car with his belongings. Soon he would be gone, and with him the activity of years of sleepovers, friendships, and comfort.

"It's funny how complete strangers can have familiar souls."

— *J. Iron Word*

He was accustomed to walking, he had done it so many times before and in so many different neighborhoods. Walking was his therapy. It was his way of clearing his head, but most of all, walking now gave him a sense of purpose where previously, it was all he knew.

He didn't want to lose sight of how far he had come, so this morning like every morning for the past two months, he pulled on his coat and wooly hat and set out to walk the same route he had walked yesterday and the day before that. Summer had turned into fall, and the blowing leaves and the arctic air sent a chill through to his bones, yet he felt warmer than he had ever felt.

He hugged his coat tighter to his chest and picked up his pace. He wanted to see Jimmy. Jimmy was his friend, a friend he didn't want to leave behind. A friend who because of circumstances, was destined to disappear into the void. He couldn't allow that to happen, not without trying with all his might to try to save his friend. He didn't know if Jimmy would be huddled in the corner of the bus shelter, underneath the cardboard box trying to keep warm. He didn't know if he would have survived the night, and he didn't know what to say.

They had once stayed at the same shelter, begged on the same street corners, and frequented the same soup kitchens. He had met Jimmy at the drop-in center a few years ago. Jimmy had shown him how to protect himself against bed bugs at the shelter, how to get a free shower at the local YMCA without anyone noticing that you didn't have a membership and how to keep your feet dry inside your shoes when it rained. Homelessness was an isolating experience, so having Jimmy as a friend and confidant made the situation tolerable.

Six months ago, as they were begging outside the coffee shop on the corner, a stranger had deposited a scratch ticket into their hat. Strangers were always dropping off the strangest items when all they really needed was money to buy a hot meal. They received bus tickets, trays of half-eaten food and once someone had left a business card, apparently the guy knew someone who knew a guy, who was hiring. They laid underneath their cardboard box that night. The shelter had been full, and they had to spend the night behind the bushes located by the hospice. Jimmy had said that he liked staying by the hospice because it made him realize that life could be worse and he could be dying.

I pulled out the hat that we used to collect the money and various other items that we had collected for the day, and there was that scratch ticket.

"Hey, Jimmy, what do you think?" I asked, holding the ticket in front of his face.

Jimmy looked at it, smiled, and closed his eyes "Go for it, if we win, use the money to buy me a nice warm fleece blanket, will ya?"

"Of course, Jimmy, of course," I remarked.

I reached into the hat, pulled out a nickel, and scratched. I was about to fold the ticket and toss it back into the hat when I realized that we had won – fifty thousand dollars. Our lives had changed right there beneath the cardboard box.

I rented us an apartment, I cleaned up, I got myself a job. I had been a professor before the downturn, but a series of unfortunate events, coupled with a constant stream of some bad luck led to unemployment, divorce and finally homelessness. I now had the opportunity to get my life on track and take Jimmy with me.

I didn't realize it at the time, but Jimmy was unable to cope with a structured life. He had a mental health illness, which now made it difficult for him to acclimate back into the workforce and society. Every job he received, he ended up losing within days for not showing up on time, or not showing up at all.

One day I came home, and Jimmy was gone. I panicked and went looking for Jimmy, and there he was nestled behind the bushes behind the hospice. I knew then, that Jimmy and I were now on different paths. I couldn't go back to living life on the streets, and Jimmy could not integrate into the life that I had missed so much – a home, a job, a bed to sleep in. I had to ensure that Jimmy would be taken care of, so I arranged for a safe deposit box in Jimmy's name and deposited half of our winnings into it. There were two keys. One I left in the safety deposit box, and the other I secured in an envelope and left with the lawyer that I had arranged to look after Jimmy's estate should anything happen to me.

I rounded the corner, and Jimmy was standing against the glass bus shelter attempting to put on a pair of well-worn black running shoes. I walked up to him, gave him a big hug, and handed him an envelope with twenty dollars. I had been giving Jimmy small amounts of money daily, to help him get through the day.

"Let me buy you lunch Jimmy," I said as I bent down and helped Jimmy put on the other shoe.

"Oh, and here, I also got you this fleece blanket to help keep you warm tonight."

Jimmy smiled and hugged me back. "Thanks, Scotty, I know it didn't work out for us on the inside, but thanks for always looking out for me."

I hugged Jimmy tighter than I think I ever had before.

"No worries, Jimmy."

I would always be there for Jimmy because Jimmy had taught me more about life and living. The truest measurement of friendship does not require money or possessions. All one needs is a cardboard box and a pair of well-worn shoes.

"She is a throwback to a time when love didn't cost a thing but was everything."

— *J. Iron Word*

The Great Depression. There was indeed nothing great about it. Yet out of the despair, hopelessness, and anguish that came from having to scrape together every last cent to feed and clothe your family, music was our escape. It was the era of swing music, big bands, blues, and jazz music.

People would save their pennies so that they could get together to go out at the end of a long hard work week and listen to sultry jazz music, the crooning of the blues, and show how we as a nation could overcome our hardships. There was no shortage of live music venues, and my favorite was jazz music. You see, jazz had a way of soothing whatever ailed you.

Oh, that jazz music, with its syncopated melodies. Jazz was like listening to poetry set to a fusion of acoustic genius. Each note clung to your skin like the warm caress of a lover's touch. It wrapped you in warmth and took you on the most wondrous of journeys. From the depth of your soul to the tips of your lips, you couldn't help but smile when jazz music tickled your eardrums. Men and women alike donned their best suits and dresses, put on their fanciest shoes, and stepped over the threshold of the speakeasy to partake in whatever their drink of choice happened to be.

Prohibition was on the rise, but listening to those singers belting out lyrics about their hardships and crooning from dimly lit stages made it all right. Somehow, life did not exist outside the speakeasy, and it was easy to forget your troubles.

"She is a gypsy with a winged soul whom the stars cannot contain; a wanderer of the universe, whose paradise is never lost, but always found beneath her feet."

— *J. Iron Word*

I had been walking for months, trying to get to freedom.

I had left my parent's house in the middle of the night and gone with the strange man that had promised my parents that I would make it to safety – to freedom. They had given him everything they had to ensure my escape, and my family did not know if I would survive, but they had to try.

The first night that we left, we didn't make it far from the village when the rebels had come to maim and torture, yet this time they did not stop with the physical abuse. They burnt down every hut in our tiny village. The strange man grabbed me and shoved me down inside a hollowed-out log that was crawling with hundreds of fire ants. Ants that proceeded to bite my bare skin and that infiltrated my clothing. I dared not scream or show any discomfort, for if the rebels had known we were there, they would have killed us too.

I could hear the screams from what had once been my home. Mothers pleading for their children, husbands begging for their families, but the rebels had no mercy. I saw them grab my mother and light her on fire right in front of my father. He buried his head in his hands, then they stabbed him in the heart. They spit on him, peed all over his bleeding body before turning the torch on his battered and disrespected body.

They danced around without showing any inkling of remorse. I scurried out of the log and tried to run back, but the man that my parents had entrusted my safety to grabbed me and covered my mouth. "Stop." He whispered with urgency. "Your parents want you to survive."

It was challenging, but I stopped struggling. Covered in fire ant bites, and tears streaming down my face, I watched as everyone and everything I had known burned as the moon began its ascent from the horizon behind my village.

"Come, let us go, we have much ground to cover."

I took the stranger's hand, and we scurried away.

That was six months ago. I looked down at the shoes that had covered so many miles and so much dangerous terrain. I was bitten, bruised, scraped, and dehydrated before we reached the railway.

"This is as far as I go. Your parents only paid me enough to take you here, the rest is up to you. You must jump onto the train once it slows down and passes by this crossing. Stay low and run fast. Grab onto the last car. The caboose is the cattle car. If you can make it onto that last car, you will be safe. The border guards hardly ever check the cattle car, but you must hide inside there nonetheless. Do not let the men see you. Here put this sweatshirt over you and keep the hood up. The men that try to jump on this train as you do are nasty, vile men that rape beautiful little girls like you. Stay safe, I will pray for you and your freedom."

He handed me a cloth bag filled with a few oranges and apples.

"How long until I make it to the border," I asked.

"Five days. Stay out of sight for five days."

"But, how will I know once I am safe? How do I know when I am across the border?"

"You will hear the men jumping, but also, the train will stop. There are no more stops from here to freedom, so do not lose track. If you do, you will be caught, and you will return."

The strange man bent down and hugged me.

"You remind me so much of my own daughter. She died two years ago attempting this very trip. Be safe."

I watched him walk off into the moonlight.

That was six months ago. I sat on the porch of the farmhouse in my bare feet. I was washing the shoes that I had left with the night that I escaped my village. The shoes that had been covered in dried dirt and cow manure from inside the last train car, and shoes that lead me down a long dusty road to the farmhouse of freedom.

There were others like me here. Men, women, and children who were all train-jumpers and who had beaten the odds and survived the ride on the freedom train. Each one of us had our own story to tell. Yet no one shared, and we all kept silent. When one person left, with an illegally obtained visa – a visa that allowed us to work in this place, undetected – another person arrived.

I placed my freshly washed shoes back on my feet. They were cold and wet, but they felt good on my hot feet. I picked up my visa and walked off the porch, guided by the moonlight. I had survived, I was free, and I was safe.

"The water that flows from her eyes is not pain; it is love."

—   *J. Iron Word*

"Today we are going to do what normal people do everywhere on Christmas," He whispered.

"I just wish this wasn't our last moment," I replied, squeezing his hand tightly.

"Don't think about it love, we have today, and that is all that should matter."

"Okay, you promised me one day of normal. A day where we don't have to think about you dying. A day where there is no such thing as cancer. A day where we will live in the moment, a moment that I will remember forever. I'm ready, show me how to live this day." I whispered back as I stared into his deep blue eyes.

He walked into the shower, and I walked over to the window seat. The one in our bedroom overlooking the rose garden below. He had proposed to me in that rose garden, and I could still smell the sweetness of the roses.

I sat down and stared out at the Autumn leaves blowing in the wind, right past the thorny stalks of the once cared for rose bushes. It had been a long time since either of us felt like cultivating the garden. The leaves twirled up and around, and at one point it appeared that a hand of leaves was stretching out to me, calling for me to join them.

I sat still, transfixed looking out at the dance of the leaves, and wondering about the afterlife. I wondered about Heaven and hell and all places in between. I wondered about what it felt like to die.

In a few short hours, this man that I had chosen to spend my life with, was wanting to end his pain and suffering. I didn't understand nor condone the decision that he decided to make. I had to respect his choice. Even if it meant that he would die peacefully in my arms.

"Come, love," he said, his pale hand outstretched.

We walked hand in hand as we descended the staircase. I released my grip when we were safely at the bottom, and my husband watched with a glimmer in his eyes as I ran toward the living room. He had decorated the entire room with a multitude of Christmas lights. Twinkling lights from every corner of the room were draped like magical lighted curtains. A Christmas tree stood in the center of the room, and the aroma from the seven-foot fir tree scented the entire space.

It was as though I had turned back the clock two years – to the night he had started to vomit blood right there beneath a Christmas tree just like the one that filled the room. I walked back over to the staircase and stopped underneath the mistletoe that he had somehow suspended from the chandelier.

He sauntered toward me and into my outstretched arms.

"How?" I asked as I buried my face into the nape of his neck.

"Normal." was all he replied.

He had been ill for so long. The last two years of our relationship were filled with doctors' appointments, chemotherapy, and radiation. Hope turned to despair, which later turned to resignation. We spent that night talking, laughing, and singing Christmas Carols. We made love beneath the Christmas tree for the last time.

At a quarter to midnight, the doorbell rang, and it was his doctor. I didn't want to let him go. I pleaded and begged. I had tried to ask him to let nature take its course and to let me be his rock and support. But I knew that there was no amount of pleading that would make him change his mind. He didn't want to continue to waste away. He didn't want to be laying in a pool of his own waste, crying out in pain and watching as I cleaned him up. He didn't want to be a burden, he had said. He would always be the love of my life, and I knew that the most selfless thing I could do would be to let him go.

I arranged the pillows on the sofa as he liked, he laid down, and I covered him with the quilt that his mother had made for us, for this occasion. He didn't want his family here, only me and the doctor. I walked over to the radio and tuned into the jazz station he loved. I returned to his side as the doctor had inserted an IV line into his arm. The tears were streaming down my face, silently and he whispered, "I love you more than life itself. Look into my eyes as I leave this earth. I want my last moment and vision to be your face."

I could not stop the tears from flowing. I must have looked horrible, but I stayed. Staring into John's eyes, and I watched as he took his final breath. The doctor put his hand on my shoulder, gave it a gentle squeeze, and left the room. All that remained was the twinkling of the lights from the Christmas tree and my sobs.

Today I stand below the mistletoe that I never could bring myself to take down, our baby asleep in my arms. Our last act of love that night produced this tiny miracle. While he is no longer with us, his memory lives on in my arms. This is normal, I thought.

"She reminds me that beauty isn't skin deep, that love is infinite and hope is a place that lives inside us."

— *J. Iron Word*

I stood patiently leaning against the old oak tree down by the river watching these lonely souls paint the beautiful sunset as it made its descent in the afternoon sky.

Many of these students were not raised with the same privilege as I had been born into, so when I finished my teaching degree, it was only natural that I wanted to teach here, in the inner city. My family had disowned me a long time ago because of my desire to teach. I was considered a servant; the lowest of the low in their eyes. I suppose that when everyone in your family came from a long line of lawyers, doctors, and politicians, anything outside that inner circle was seen as the ultimate betrayal.

I watched my students paint dramatic landscapes of fiery red, blazing orange, and vibrant yellow skies. Each one capturing their own interpretation of the wonders of the setting sun into the riverbank. Elijah's painting, however, caught my eye. Like his bright purple sneakers, Elijah had used different hues of purple with a sliver of orange to represent what he saw. I walked up behind him and placed my hand on his shoulder. Elijah had been born into poverty and to add insult to injury, he had been born without arms. No one expected him to live, but he defied the odds. I had remembered Elijah as a baby. His parents would bring him to my father's clinic for his monthly check-ups. I watched as all the other patients in the clinic moved far away from Elijah's parents as though they thought that being born without arms was somehow contagious. People could be so cruel.

"Hi Mrs. Dyer, can I play with him?" I would ask each and every time. I wanted them to know that not all people were as judgmental as the people that attended my father's clinic.

Mrs. Dyer would smile, and she would place Elijah on the floor in front of me. I would rattle the plastic toy keys and squeeze the rubber ducky in front of his face. Elijah would squeal with delight. For a kid who didn't have arms, he was the happiest baby I had ever met. As Elijah grew older, he didn't lose his joy. He seemed to exude it more, and he had such a positive outlook on life.

Elijah turned to me and said, "Everyone paints what they see, I choose to paint the beauty that could be. There is so much potential in everything Jana." Elijah smiled and turned back to the easel, picked up his paintbrush with his mouth, and continued to paint broad, hope-filled strokes.

"I caught myself smiling thinking of a memory we have yet to make; I'll let you know when we get there."

— *J. Iron Word*

He sat on the subway, holding a bag of doughnuts. An innocent act and quite normal to the naked eye, but this bag of doughnuts signified strength.

A few years ago, he would not have been able to look at a doughnut, let alone show any restraint. Eating one doughnut would have led to eating three doughnuts, then four, and before he could comprehend what was happening, the whole box of doughnuts would have been consumed, and he would have found himself bent over the toilet vomiting every ounce of sugary goodness that was in the pit of his stomach. He would have felt ashamed and defeated by his lack of restraint. This would have led to more binging on his commute home, followed by another purge session once he arrived at his home.

His wife suspected something was wrong, but he had become a master of deception. He lied about having developed stomach ulcers, his job as a trader was stressful don't you know, followed by a stomach bug of some sort, these lies were his comfort and his escape from what he

47

knew was wrong. Yet it had become more comfortable and easier to lie and explain away his problem. Of course, at the time, he didn't think he had a problem. Food was his crutch. When he was upset, he ate, when he was sad, he ate, when he was happy he ate more. It was a vicious cycle that he could not break until that night.

He had been walking home after another long day on the trading floor. He crossed the intersection of fifth and main and caught a glimpse of himself in the shoe store window. He looked pale, gaunt, and sick. Dark circles were encircling his eyes, his cheekbones were sunken in, and his fingers were bony.

What had happened to him? Why did he look so ill? It looked like he was on death's door. How had he not noticed it before? He crumpled to the ground crying. He summoned up enough strength to call his wife, who promptly came to pick him up. When they arrived home, Jessica sat holding him on the sofa and stroking his hair. He told her everything. He told her about the binging, the purging. He apologized for not being there for her the way a husband should be there for his wife. Jessica just held him.

The next morning, he called in sick to work, saw his physician, and took a six-month sabbatical. He vowed to change his life. He promised to live the life that he had been given and not to take anything else for granted. He joined a gym, he started seeing a behavioral counselor, and he bought himself a brand-new pair of brown leather running shoes.

Now here he sat on the subway, his brown leather running shoes shining, and he was holding a bag of doughnuts. He was thankful for his wife and grateful that his co-workers were now celebrating his return. He was now binge and purge free. *One day at a time*, he thought, one day at a time.

"Let us unlock the skeletons in our closets and bury them together."

– *J. Iron Word*

My home was the North.

North of sixty is what I heard the pale faces say when I was a little girl. The pale faces always came onto the reserve every few months. They would arrive wearing expensive-looking suits, and they all had well-manicured hands. *Did they not work?* I had thought. The men on the reserve had dirt embedded beneath their fingertips. Hands that were dirt-stained and rough from working on the land. Our men hunted, they fished, and they built fires.

At least once a year these pale faces would meet with the Chief who dutifully drove them around. The pale faces had wanted to meet with us, the Chief had said. They tried to understand our Northern life, where the trees grew to be only four feet tall, where when it snowed, iced roads were made to bring food in from down south, and where the northern lights danced their magical dance across the frigid arctic sky. The pale faces never stayed long, but they returned like clockwork every year.

Kôkum would say that the pale faces wanted to keep us under their thumbs just like they had done when she was a child. Kôkum had been ripped away from her family when she was just my age. She was forced to forget her heritage and stripped of her culture. They forbade Kôkum from speaking the language of her people. She was forced to learn French and English. If she were caught disobeying the rules of the pale faces, she would be punished.

Kôkum lived in those residential schools run mainly by the pale faces for five years. When the residential schools closed, she was returned home. Home, however, had a different meaning, because she now felt like an outsider. She did not know her parents or the siblings that had come after her. When her mother would make bannock and had asked her to help, she did not know what to do because she did not know what ingredients to gather.

It was at that moment Kôkum said that she had decided that she was going to spend every waking hour re-learning the culture that she was forced to forget. She had passed what she was able to learn onto her children and grandchildren for she did not want us to forget our ancestors and where we came from.

Kôkum taught us which berries were edible and which ones were not meant to be eaten. She showed us how herbs were to be used for healing, and we spent many hours in the grand lodge listening to her, and the other elders tell us stories of magnificent animals and spirits, all of which were meant to teach us the lessons of our people.

"Don't ever forget, my girl." She would say to me, and she would make me promise to pass on our heritage to the next generation.

Today, I sit around a Formica table at the local community Centre teaching the pale faces how to make Mukluks – one of the very traditions that the pale faces had tried to erase from my people. I watch as they bead their designs on their own boots, and I charge money to do so. With the money that I earn from teaching our art, I have created a fund that will allow the next generation of North of Sixty youths to achieve independence – independence from the pale faces.

"She is dangerous because she knows what she is capable of."

— *J. Iron Word*

"Hello?"

"Pack up bitch we're going to Europe" The voice on the other end of the phone screeched.

Of course, that level of both enthusiasm and vulgarity could only emanate from one person, Darcy.

"Hello to you too, Darcy," I said matter-of-factly.

"Yeah, yeah, listen we don't have much time, give me your credit card number, I'm booking us a flight to London."

"Seriously? Who is *us*, and when are we going?" I asked, amused.

"We are – You, me, Jules, Lexie, and Flavia-five gorgeous girls are about to get shit-faced overseas this September long weekend. Come on, give me your credit card, my travel agent isn't going to hold the seats forever. I've already called the rest of the girls, and they're all in."

"Darcy, you know I'm still a starving student with a part-time job as a greeter at the Disney Store, my credit is nonexistent, so I don't have a credit card."

"Come on Katia, you have to come, it won't be the same without you" Darcy pleaded.

"Well, I still have Jeff's credit card. Do you think my ticket will process on his card?"

"Yes! Give me the jerk's credit card number, and I'll book your ticket. Honestly Katia I really don't know what you're still doing with him. He's cheated on you so many times it's embarrassing."

"I know, I know. Screw it, here's the number. I'll figure out how to pay it back later." I said as I pulled Jeff's gold card from the cardboard box inside my wardrobe.

"Perfect. Look we're all going to Limelight tonight, pick me up around seven, okay? Toodles." The phone went dead.

I smiled as I placed the cordless phone back in its cradle. Darcy and I had become fast friends. It was only a few short months ago that I was introduced to her at Go-Go's; one of the hottest nightclubs in the city. Mr. Asshole, as Jeff is now affectionately called by the girls, was schmoozing fellow bouncers, and I had become bored with listening to his narcissistic stories, so I wandered over to the bar for a drink. Out of nowhere, a girl with the curliest mop of brown hair jumped on my back. I panicked and flipped her skinny ass onto the cold concrete floor. Turns out that crazy girl was my old high school friend Flavia.

I hadn't seen her in over three years. Four weeks later, her group of friends and I had become inseparable. Not bad for an ugly duckling such as myself. I really didn't consider myself ugly – just dull. I was never the type of girl that made guys stop dead in their tracks. I was funny-or so I was told – and I was smart, but I was always that girl on the sidelines looking in, and thanks to these crazy girls, for the first time in what seemed like forever, I belonged. I was having the time of my life.

Darcy was right, I really could not figure out why I was still with Jeff. The sex was not good. Actually, it was downright awful, but he was gorgeous, and he filled a void. I'm not quite sure what void I was looking to fill, but while I figured it out, it didn't hurt to have a piece of eye candy on my arm. I guess in a sense I was using him as much as he was using me.

I returned Jeff's gold card to its hiding place and looked around the dark basement apartment. I had spent too much time wallowing in self-pity. I was ready for my next adventure, and I knew that I would find it with these ladies in tow. Perhaps I would meet a stranger who would make me the center of his universe for a change. I pulled out my suede high heel boots and a pair of skinny jeans and marched myself into the shower to get ready for a night to remember and perhaps even the time of my life.

"She's the perfect storm, the kind of woman that makes you believe love lives in lightning bolts."

—   *J. Iron Word*

I sat on top of the dryer at the laundromat three doors down from my apartment in Venice Beach, California. I was scrolling through Kijiji on my smartphone searching for another job. I was currently a server at Joey's diner on the corner, but I needed a job that was going to pay me a little more money and a job that would allow me the flexibility to pursue my dream of skating in the roller derby on the weekends. It was a silly dream, but it was my dream, nonetheless.

I had moved to California from the colony. I had been born into the colony and had spent the majority of my life there. We were simple people, with simple values and who lived a simple way of life, but for as long as I could remember, I wanted excitement, an excitement that you could not find in the confines of the colony. Those who lived apart from the colony were Satan worshippers, damned to spend eternity in hell. Fire and brimstone were a natural consequence of living in the modern outside world.

Father made the mistake of making me a pair of metal roller-skates when I was five. He said he hoped it would help me dispel my boundless energy. He was right. I spent my days skating around the colony as I completed my chores, and it seemed like my mother was constantly applying her homemade salve to my growing number of bruises and scrapes nightly.

When I turned eleven, my father had an outsider as a customer who had given him a pair of roller-skates because as he said, he felt sorry for me and my tattered strap-on metal skates. From that moment I was in love. I knew that one day, I would leave the colony and pursue a career in roller skating. Of course, when I told father and mother this, they scoffed and said that if I ever left, I would never be allowed back in and that I too would spend eternity burning in the fiery pit of hell.

The only person that I could confide in was Isaac. Isaac was my soul mate. He was strong, handsome, and I had been promised to be his wife when I turned sixteen. I really didn't mind that my parents had chosen Isaac as my husband, I did love him. He treated me as an equal. He wasn't like the other men in our colony. He didn't believe that men held blue jobs and women had pink jobs and that men's roles and women's roles were never to be traded. Isaac helped me make bread, and I helped Isaac build fences. We were a perfect pair. I tried to convince Isaac to run away with me when we turned sixteen.

"Miriam, you know that I love you and that I would do anything for you, but I belong here in the colony. My family depends on me."

"I know Isaac, but what about us? If you're worried about work, don't be Isaac. You are the best carpenter I know. You could build houses. You certainly are singlehandedly responsible for building many of the houses here in the colony," I coaxed "I don't know what I will do on the outside without you."

"Miriam, I love you for your endless faith in me. You are the smartest, most determined person I know. You don't need me to survive, you will survive all on your own."

"I know that Isaac, but I want you with me."

Isaac would kiss my nose and tell me that everything would be all right and that I would be fine and that if the good Lord willed it, we would be together, although he could not imagine that was what the Lord had wanted for him.

On my sixteenth birthday, I snuck away in the middle of the night. I had saved a total of two thousand dollars from selling eggs at the market. Isaac had given me over ten thousand dollars, money he had made from his carpentry work with the outsiders. We hugged at the edge of the colony, and I didn't look back.

That was three years ago. I had often wondered what had become of Isaac. You see, as soon as boys and girls in the colony turn sixteen, they are mandated to marry. Isaac and I were to be married the next day. I loved him, and he knew that, but he loved me enough to keep my secret and allow me to leave in the middle of the night.

I arrived in California full of hopes and dreams. I skated every now and again, and I was so good that I was invited to join the circuit. The problem was that I had to make some more money before I could enjoy my passion. I blew a big bubble with the gum that I had been chewing and jumped down from the top of the dryer. I started to mindlessly remove my laundry from the dryer, my mind once again floated back to thoughts of Isaac.

I wrote Isaac several letters over the years, but I was unsure as to whether any of those letters had been delivered. If they were, did he receive them, or did they fall into the hands of his parents who would have thrown them away, without any mention to him? Once you left the colony, you were shunned, and no communication was allowed. I knew this, but I had to tell Isaac about my life.

We had shared everything since we were five. I was standing folding my clothes when I dropped my roller derby sock on the floor. I bent down to pick it up, and from the corner of my eye, in the back corner of the laundromat, I saw a familiar pair of black boots. I turned around, and there in the back corner was Isaac.

"Isaac!" I squealed.

The little old lady in the corner, who had been sleeping, waiting for her own washing to finish stirred but she did not wake.

"What are you doing here?" I said as I skated over toward him.

"Miriam, life in the colony was not the same without you. I had to leave. I am thankful that you had sent those letters all these years."

"You got them?" I asked, stunned.

"It wasn't easy Miriam, father almost caught me reading them. I suppose it was faith that one of my chores was to fetch the mail; otherwise, I would have thought that you had forgotten me all these years."

"Isaac, I could never forget you," I said, and I threw my arms around him and hugged him close to me. I had missed his arms. I missed his scent, and most of all, I missed how safe and secure he had always managed to make me feel.

"I missed you, Isaac."

"Miriam, I missed you too" He whispered softly into my ear.

Isaac kissed my nose and it was at that moment that I knew that all my dreams had come true.

"…What's in a name but a million memories that can never be forgotten…"

— *J. Iron Word*

"Eeny meeny miny moe, catch a tiger by the toe, if he hollers let him go, Eeny meeny miny moe – You're it Alex."

"Aww come on guys, I'm always it," Alex whined.

"Yeah well, you always stand in the same place, we can't help it." Greg laughed.

"Whatever guys, fine. I'm it, go hide, and I'll find you jerks just like I always do."

"Sore loser" We all yelled in unison as we ran away.

We had all met as kids at camp Muskoka when we were nine. This was to be our last year here. We had been summertime friends for the past four years, and somehow, we had formed a bond. We all kept in touch throughout the school year, and we all looked forward to reuniting in the summer.

When June hit, it was as if we had never been apart. Like somehow, we were all connected. We had vowed that we would be friends forever. Forever was a long time when you were thirteen, and it had been easy to keep in touch up until that point. However, with each passing year, camp

Muskoka became a distant memory. Sure we kept in touch for the first year, but as junior high turned into high school and high school turned into university, it became increasingly difficult to stay on top of the letter writing and the phone calls.

By the time we all graduated with whatever degree each one of us had been pursuing, our childhood friendship was a distant memory. I sat at my desk looking out at the lake wondering whatever happened to those guys that I spent my summers with. Did Alex, the debater, become a lawyer? Perhaps Kelan finally found his calling as a comedian. He always had a way of making us laugh. Graham was the quiet one, and we all joked that he would become a scientist, concocting the cure for whatever disease needed curing.

The years passed by, and I didn't know what had become of the best group of friends that I had ever known. I was headed to Kenya on assignment. I had become a photojournalist, and I had been sent on a variety of jobs all around the globe to take pictures of the stories that everyone thought were newsworthy. I was responsible for documenting the life of Marines in Afghanistan, and I was there when the world trade center came crashing down. I was not on assignment during that sad time, but I did manage to capture some very riveting photographs. I was not a writer, but my pictures told the stories. Every tear, every smile, the vacant eyes, it all meant something, just as my friendship with those guys said something.

As I dug around in my office drawer looking for my passport, I pulled out the one photo that I had of the old gang. We had gathered in a circle, on our last day at camp and Morgan got the idea to take a picture of our feet. He never said why, but it seemed like a good idea at the time. A few weeks after that, this picture arrived in my mailbox, and I have carried it ever since. I grabbed my beaten leather duffle bag and my passport and walked out onto the front steps to wait for the taxi that I had reserved the night before.

I was heading out for another assignment, but I had very few details, which was not the norm. I usually knew where I was flying to and who I was to meet, however this time I didn't know who had requested me. All I knew was that the person had asked for me specifically. My editor seemed quite elusive when I started to inquire more about the assignment. I figured it was a dignitary or some high-profile politician and that this assignment had to remain confidential for security reasons. I watched as the taxi pulled up, on time and before I could take my first step, four guys jumped out. They looked familiar, but I couldn't place them.

"Alright gentlemen, I'm Connor, where are we headed and what's my assignment," I asked, handing my duffle bag to the first guy.

They looked at each other and laughed. The group walked toward me and placed their feet in a circle beside mine. All our toes touching.

*"When she dies someone will throw her ashes in the sky,
so she can live with the stars where she belongs."*

— *J. Iron Word*

July thirteenth was the worst day of my life. Literally no joke. It was a Friday, trust me the irony is not lost on me, but that is where my story begins.

It had been a long hard day at the shelter. Men, women, and children all homeless kept filtering in, in record numbers. It was challenging to sit and listen to story after story of heartache, yet day in and day out that's what I did. Sometimes I thought that was all they wanted, someone who would genuinely listen and not judge.

There was so much judgment in the world. If you were hooked on one illicit drug or another, you were an addict. If you were homeless, you were good for nothing and lazy. It wasn't easy to see a whole segment of society labeled, stigmatized, and treated like second-class citizens. Yet here they were; the ejected, the tossed aside, the forgotten. What people and society, in general, failed to realize, was that these people were somebody's mother, father, sister, brother, and grandchildren, and they had no control over their life circumstances. Life had shoveled a big steaming hot pile of shit on their doorstep, and they were just trying to climb over it and get to the other side.

As I said, it wasn't easy to listen to these stories of heartache, especially when I knew that at the end of my day, I was one of the lucky ones who had a warm house and a freshly made bed to retire to. I didn't have to wonder if tonight would be the night that I didn't get a bed and would have to resort to huddling under the bridge, next to the burning fire in the trash barrel trying to stay warm. I was exhausted, mentally exhausted, but I didn't want to give up hope. Hope that every one of those individuals at the shelter would one day have a bed of their own to enjoy. They would find a job – and keep it, they would rent an apartment with their very own shower, and they would watch their children graduate from school instead of watching them beg for bus fare on the street corner.

As I placed the key in the lock of my front door, I wondered how many other times I had turned this key without thinking about how much this small gesture meant. I stepped inside and went straight up to my bathroom to draw a hot bath, hoping that the steam from the hot water would somehow cleanse away the despair that I felt in my bones. I opened my closet, and it hit me.

Shoes, I had so many pairs of shoes. When did I turn into Imelda Marcos I thought? There were running shoes and heels, winter boots of varying lengths, even slippers that still had the tags on them. Above these shoes were rows upon rows of unworn t-shirts. I was a hoarder. I was living in excess when the very people that I was trying to help were living with nothing. I shook my head in disgust. I ran back to the bathroom, stopped the bath, and started to bag up all the t-shirts that were hanging above. I found another bag and flung shoes, boots, and slippers into the bag. In the end, I had four huge garbage bags filled with items from my closet that I didn't wear.

I jumped back into my car and drove back to the shelter. I walked up to the first person I saw and asked them if I could trade their old shirt for one of my new ones. The guy who looked like Mr. Claus was more than happy to oblige. He took off his dirty, AC/DC shirt with the holes in the back and handed it to me. I shoved it in a separate bag and gave him a new one from my other bag. He smelled it and smiled.

"Smells like cherries," and he put it on.

I moved on to the next person, then another, and before I knew it, I had supplied shirts for nearly fifty people. Then came the shoes. I knew that it would be harder to trade in – especially the heels but anyone with a size eight foot was welcome to take a pair. I was shocked at how many people actually wore a size eight in shoes. When all the excitement settled, I was left with four full bags of old trade-ins and half a bag of items that I had brought.

"Thank you, miss," said the little girl with the pigtails wearing one of my t-shirts. The shirt that her mother had chosen for her was too big and fit her like a dress.

"You're welcome. I'm sorry, what's your name, darling?"

"Chelsea."

"Well then Chelsea, that t-shirt and those running shoes match well together."

She was wearing the most fascinating running shoes with faces designed on them.

"Thanks, my mom found these on the street. They have a hole on the bottom, but I put a piece of cardboard inside to help keep my feet dry. Of course, when it rains, I have to change the cardboard a lot."

"Oh my…I wished I had a pair of shoes in here that would fit you."

"Oh, that's okay, I like these shoes anyway. I don't think that I would get rid of them even if you did have a pair of shoes to fit me."

"Oh, okay," I laughed. "That shirt is so large on you. Do you want me to see if I have a smaller one?"

"NO!" she yelled.

"Oh dear, I'm sorry Chelsea, did I upset you? I'm not going to take that shirt away from you."

"Sorry, it's just that I had seen this exact shirt last week when Mom went to the recycle bin. I fell in love with it right away, but Mom didn't have enough money to buy it. That's the thing I hate the most. Mom says that the Recycle Bin is a store that helps people like us, people down on their luck, but I don't understand why they charge for the clothes and other stuff they have there. People like us don't have very much money – right?"

"Yes, I suppose," I replied in awe at the wisdom of such a young child.

"Well, why then do they try to charge us for items that we need? It should be free?"

"Good question, Chelsea, I do not know." I stared at her perplexed.

"Well, I don't care now. I will have this shirt for a long time, and I will be able to grow into it."

"Yes, you surely will," I said, as Chelsea walked away.

She had a point. And that is when the idea for the community closet came to life.

With my boyfriend's help, I emptied the wardrobe that I had in my bedroom and drove it to the community garden across from the shelter. I placed all the remaining items I had in the community closet and left a note that read – *Take what you need and leave what you can.*

Today marks one year since that day. There are now five community closets scattered around the city where people can leave items of use – shoes, blankets, socks, coats, and t-shirts for the homeless or someone in need. And the homeless reciprocate by leaving their old dirty items, that I retrieve, launder, and replace.

"Our physical appearance is the smallest part of us, but somehow it is all that people see."

— *J. Iron Word*

Acceptance. Life is about acceptance.

Life is about waking up each and every morning no matter where in the world you live, breathing in a big deep breath, and releasing positivity into the universe. Life is about looking in the mirror and realizing that you're a survivor.

Life is about thinking outside the box, living on the edge, and being a fucking unicorn in a world that tries to keep you confined to a stereotype.

I had always known that somehow, I was different. At the time, I couldn't put my finger on it or pinpoint the exact reason why I didn't feel comfortable in my own skin, but there was always this *feeling*.

My first clue surfaced the year I turned five. My mother had innocently enrolled me in dance lessons to help with my lack of coordination. I was so excited. My parents had argued for three days straight because as I recall, my father's exact words were that only girls took dance lessons and that no boy of his was going to go traipsing around on a stage in some feminine attire. I cried for the three days after my parents stopped fighting. My father had won this battle, and Mom quickly made a phone call to Ms. Tandy's Dance Emporium with the excuse that I was too shy to attend. Really? I was too shy?

However, the exact moment that I knew beyond a shadow of a doubt that which I could not name at the time occurred on my tenth birthday. My parents did not have a lot of money and were somewhat thrifty except for when it came to my birthday. They could never afford to throw me a birthday party, but my mother always managed to scrape together enough money for an outing at the mall.

We would walk, talk, laugh, and have lunch at the food court. She always had just a cup of tea while I was allowed to order anything I wanted. I usually had a burger and fries followed by a chocolate-dipped Dairy Queen ice cream cone. This day Mom mentioned that I could pick out a new pair of running shoes as my special birthday gift. I was elated. I usually got to choose a small toy or t-shirt that was on sale. Shoes were typically reserved for the beginning of the school year luxury.

We walked over to the sports store, and I ran inside, excited to pick out a new pair of shoes. I looked up and down the wall covered in the latest running shoes. Most were for running or basketball, two things I did not partake in. I guess you could say that I was not a very sport-inclined kid. Then there they were. Halfway down the wall on the middle shelf in all their colorful glory.

"Mom," I asked, "Can I try these on?" I asked, pointing to the exact shoes that had my full attention.

"Evan, those are girls' shoes," my mother replied.

In that instant, I knew.

I had felt different because I was different. Every time I looked in the mirror, I noticed the mismatch. I was a boy on the outside, but on the inside, every fiber of my being screamed something different. Why had I been born trapped inside the body of a boy? Why had God played this cruel joke on me? Were there other boys who felt this same torture, or was I the only one? I too wanted long hair. I wanted to be able to apply lipstick and nail polish as my mother did every Sunday night without being ridiculed and being called a candy-assed pansy by my own father.

"Evan what's wrong?" Mom asked as I stood with tears streaming down my face.

"I'm a girl mom, not a boy, A GIRL!" I shouted. "I want these shoes, not the shoes over there in the boy section. These shoes are colorful. They have all these different people on them all living side by side in all their different forms. Happy. United."

Everyone stopped and stared. I saw mom's face flush, and I thought that she was going to get angry or worse. But my kind, patient, loving mother did not get mad. She walked close to me, kneeled down, and hugged me so tight that I thought she would break a few of my ribs. She looked me straight in the eyes, wiped my face and stood up and asked the salesperson who was standing there, jaw open, to bring me a pair of those shoes in size five. What happened after was pure love and acceptance. My mother took me to her nail salon for my first pedicure. I painted my nails bright pink and never looked back. I love you, Mom.

Love Evie (Not Evan).

"When we are born no one is there to tell us our lives have begun, but we live anyway. Somewhere along the way we learn to be careful and plan, forgetting to press 'start' on living."

— *J. Iron Word*

Every day for the past ten years he pulled on his high-top running shoes and made the same walk to the bus stop on the corner to catch the five-fifteen bus so he could make it into work on time for seven-thirty. He was once so full of excitement and energy, but now walking out the door had become a chore.

He disliked his life, well not his life exactly, merely his job and especially his boss. His boss was, for lack of a better term, a battle ax. She was the type of person who when he arrived at work late, would not say a word but would ask her cronies to address the matter. She had sayings that he felt were demeaning to people in general and her catchphrase 'Not my Problem' was one that every time he heard it, he wanted to ram straight down her unsympathetic neck. He stood inside the bus shelter, hands in his pocket, and looked down at his battered running shoes.

Fitting, he thought.

These running shoes which had been a constant in his trek to work every day looked how he felt. Battered, torn, and scuffed. These shoes kept his feet dry, but they were merely packaging around vulnerable socked feet. Just as his work was the wrapping that kept his life contained. He had once enjoyed his job, but he could now say beyond a shadow of a doubt that he no longer felt the same enjoyment and enthusiasm as he had a few years ago. He knew his feelings were really not about the job, his role, or the myriad of tasks that he had to complete daily, but rather about the constant game of having to outmaneuver his boss. He had to continually be one step ahead of her because she found fault with everything.

He hated the previous CEO for resigning four years ago because ever since that fateful day his life changed and he had become a frazzled mess. He often compared his position as Vice President of Operations at Millennium International to working in a silo. He often wondered how teams at Google, Apple, and Microsoft managed to inspire their leaders – what was that moxie they had that his current environment was lacking. Or perhaps he lacked? His wife begged him daily to quit, to move on, but a little thing called a mortgage, children, and failure were words that turned around in his head on a perpetual loop.

Today as he stood waiting for the number 444 bus – the same bus that he rode daily for the past ten years. He had an epiphany, *That's it*, he thought. He had become just as grumpy at work as the bus driver on the number 444 bus. His daily routine had become a routine that lacked inspiration. He complained daily and cried silently every night. Something had to change. He had to change. He looked down at his running shoes, and in that instant, he realized that these running shoes no longer served their purpose and were, in reality, merely a means to an end. As the bus approached, stopped, and opened its doors, he smiled, bent down, and took off his running shoes.

"Hey, buddy you getting on?" yelled the ruddy-faced bus driver with his usual scowl.

"Nope I'm good," he replied back.

He placed the running shoes beside the bus shelter for some deserving soul and walked back home on his socked feet.

End

Permissions

All quotes courtesy of J. Iron Word from published works.

Abstract Heart. J. Iron Word, 2016. Monarch Publishing.
Live Loud, Love Loud., J. Iron Word, 2018, Iron Society
LLC.
She is Me. J. Iron Word, 2019, Iron Society LLC.